FLY GUY MEETS FLY GIRL!

Tedd Arnold

Cartwheel
B·O·O·K·S ®

SCHOLASTIC INC.
New York   Toronto   London   Auckland
Sydney   Mexico City   New Delhi   Hong Kong

For Elizabeth (Lizzz!) and Cortney
—T.A.

Copyright © 2010 by Tedd Arnold.

Library of Congress Cataloging-in-Publication Data is available.

Arnold, Tedd.
Fly Guy meets Fly Girl / by Tedd Arnold.
p. cm.
Summary: When Fly Guy meets Fly Girl, he is amazed and smitten.
ISBN 978-0-545-11029-7
[1. Flies--Fiction.] I. Title.
PZ7.A7379Fl 2010   [E]--dc22
2009014182

ISBN 978-0-545-11029-7

10 9 8 7 6 5 4 3 2   10 11 12 13 14

Printed in Singapore 46
First printing, January 2010

A boy had a pet fly.
He named him Fly Guy.
Fly Guy could say
the boy's name—

BUZZ!

Chapter 1

One day, Buzz and
Fly Guy were bored.
Fly Guy said,

FUNZZIE?

"Yeah," said Buzz.
"Let's do something fun."

Buzz and Fly Guy
went for a walk.

They played chase.

They cooled off
in the fountain.

A girl was running.
A fly was chasing her.

"Don't worry," said Buzz.
"Flies aren't pests.
They are pets."

"I know," said the girl.
"This is my pet.
Her name is Fly Girl."

Chapter 2

Buzz said, "This is Fly Guy. He can do tricks."

"Fly Girl can do tricks, too!"
said the girl.

"Fly Guy eats gross stuff,"
said Buzz.

"Fly Girl eats grosser stuff!" said the girl.

"Fly Guy can say my name," said Buzz.

BUZZ!

"Fly Girl can say my name, too!"
said the girl.

"Do you want to play
on the swings?" said Buzz.
"Sure," said Liz.

Chapter 3

Fly Guy and Fly Girl
sat side by side.

Fly Guy said,

WUZZLE
WUZZLE

That is fly talk for
"You are nice."

Fly Girl said,

That is fly talk for
"You are nice, too."

Fly Guy and Fly Girl
talked and talked.

WUZZLE WUZZLE

WUZZLE
WUZZY

WUZZY WUZZLE WUZZA WUZZLE

WUZZLE WUZZLE

WUZZY WUZZA

Then Fly Guy said,

And Fly Girl said,

Fly Guy and Fly Girl both said,

WUZZLE WUZZZUP!

That is fly talk for
"Let's be friends."

"See you soon,"
said Buzz and Liz.

"Yeah," said Buzz.
"That was fun!"